I0699816

Working Blue Press

First Edition

ISBN 978-1-967038-09-1 (Kindle)
ISBN 978-1-967038-10-7 (Print)

For all the women who love good sex,
and all the meals you've eaten while
talking about it with good friends.

Content

Suggestions for Further Reading

Girls Who Brunch Erotic Series
Books 1, 2, 3 and 4.

Follow Lacey Love on Amazon to keep abreast of new releases!

Scrambler Platter

Girls Who Brunch Erotic Series

1

Scrambler Platter

"Tucker-mother-fucker-Brand."

Tabitha smiled with triumph as she slid seductively into the gold booth at the high-end restaurant in downtown Cleveland on a gorgeous fall day. She gave her three brunch companions a shit-eating grin that begged for them to ask her about her silver fox.

"That name seems like it should be on a billboard somewhere," Summer quipped.

"A 'wanted' billboard or a 'real estate' billboard?" Annie questioned.

"Definitely 'wanted,'" Fawn said.

They all smiled at Tabitha as the waiter sauntered up in his black bowtie and crisp white shirt. "May I get you a drink, Miss?"

"Miss? Oh, big tip for you, honey," Tabitha said. She turned to face him, her heaving breasts almost popping out of her sleek, black, calf-length Vera Wang that made her plus-size curves pop. "I want a tequila, straight up."

"I'll be right out with it," he said. He flicked a sexy eyebrow at her and walked away as Tabitha turned back to the ladies.

"Don't be jealous of me, bitches," she said as her long, black fingernails clicked the table, a five-karat yellow diamond bauble dancing on the middle finger of her right hand.

"Holy shit, what's that?" Summer grabbed Tabitha's hand as they all leaned in and took in the sparkling beauty.

"I told you already. Tucker-mother-fucker-Brand." And with

that, Tabitha let out a joyful squeal that made them all laugh, as everyone near them turned and laughed with them.

"Holy shit, I need this story," Annie bantered.

"No, not yet," Tabitha said. She pulled her diamond back and glanced generously at each of them. "I'm going to talk the whole time about my hot, sexy fox, so first, all of you give your updates and then, it's my turn."

She turned her attention to Fawn. "Are you pregnant yet, gorgeous, because I see juice with no alcohol in front of you?"

Fawn blushed under Tabitha's stare as her platinum hair, now shoulder-length, tickled her bare shoulders in a seductive strapless, red number.

"P.S. you're looking hot as fuck. Stanny must be a happy man."

"Tabitha, stop," Fawn drawled as she tucked a hair behind her ear. "And yes, he is."

The four of them giggled as Fawn spilled her news. "I *am* pregnant."

Another round of squeals that brought the attention of the whole restaurant as the girls hugged and cheered.

"Oh, I can't wait for this little fucker," Tabitha squealed. "Witchy, bitchy, Auntie Tabitha is throwing the baby shower. When are you due?"

"May 10," Fawn said. She shrugged her shoulders with happiness. "We'll know in a couple months if it's a boy or girl."

"Oh, Fawn, this is so wonderful," Annie cooed. "I hope it's a little girl."

"Me, too," Summer said. "So happy for you guys."

"You've got news, too, Summer, yes?" Fawn asked. "Did I hear a little rumor about you moving?"

Summer's bright white smile lit up as she rubbed her hands together in happiness, her strappy yellow dress making her brown eyes look gold. "Yes, you did. Ace asked me to move in with him and I said yes."

"Oh honey," Tabitha said. She clapped her hands together. "This is fantastic. When is the housewarming so I can buy you something amazing?"

"We're moving into his place in two weeks," she said. "Party is two weeks after that. You all are, obviously, invited."

"Ace is awesome, Summer," Annie said. "You two are perfect together, honestly."

"Thanks," Summer said. They all glanced at Annie as she dipped her head down and her blonde

locks fell over her shoulders. Her
cap-sleeve turquoise, body-hugging
dress fit perfectly and made her
green eyes shine.

"Honey," Tabitha said. "Did
Christopher move out already?"

Annie nodded as she looked up
at them with misty eyes. She shook
them off and took a sip of her
drink.

"You and Tommy doin' okay?"
Fawn asked.

"We're okay," Annie said.
"Right now, we're just labeling it
'as taking a break,' but…who
knows?"

"But you and Tommy are still
together, right?" Summer asked.

"Tommy and I are forever,"
Annie said. She touched the
diamond necklace at her throat.
"But we loved Christopher, and we
thought it might work, but…it was
harder than we thought."

"I'm sorry," Summer said.

"Me, too," Tabitha said. She rubbed Annie's shoulder.

"Me, three," Fawn added.

They all nodded quietly.

"Today is not about me," Annie said. She bucked up and smiled. "Today is about Tucker-mother-fucker-Brand."

"Yes!" Summer laughed as they all turned to Tabitha.

Tabitha couldn't help the smile on her face as she took center stage.

"Ladies, he has the most magnificent penis I've ever seen."

"Oh shit, this is brunch, baby!" Summer laughed as the waiter returned, placed the tequila in front of Tabitha, and took out his pad to take their orders.

"What can I get for you?"

"Oh, honey," Tabitha said. "I'll take the Scrambler Platter."

"Scrambler Platter?" Annie asked.

"That's got a little bit of everything," Summer answered.

"Oh," said Tabitha. She glanced at her friends. "You have no idea."

"Holy hell," Fawn said. "Talk."

As the ladies put in their orders, Tabitha sipped her tequila and started telling them about her million-dollar client, the silver fox, who was now her part-time lover.

2

The Client

Tabitha sashayed into the high-end salon with all the gusto of a powerful woman ready for business. She was the Steel of Steel & Grace Salons, as well as one of its top-rated stylists. They only served million-dollar clients and had staked their reputation on it. They used the finest of everything, from styling tools to make-up, and created an atmosphere for these—often celebrity— clients that was second to none.

"Grace," she purred as she walked into the main office. Grace, a forty-year-old wife of three and married for twenty years, was a gorgeous specimen to look at, as well as a top-shelf human being.

Today her look was safari, with three-inch, beige Manolo Blahniks, Army green joggers cinched at her waist, a cream-colored halter top, and tons of gold jewelry.

"Tabs," she purred back. She winked. "You've got a surprise client this morning. Lucky you're early. And looking hot."

"Oh, really?" Tabitha sat her coffee down. She smoothed down her hot cinnamon red slinky dress that hugged every delicious curve of her body and clicked her heels twice. "Who is it?"

"A silver fox. Name's Tucker. Tucker Brand. Multi-millionaire. Specializes in sports teams and the stock market. He's hot."

"Sounds like just my type." Tabitha winked at Grace and did a little twerk of her hips before grabbing her tools. "Where is this silver god?"

"I put him in the private room for you."

"Oh, you know how much I love the private room," Tabitha said smoothly. "Do not disturb."

"No promises."

Tabitha laughed as she sauntered toward one of the private suites in the back of the salon. It was one of their selling points. Big money clients could come here for peace and quiet, assured that no fan or business owner looking for an investment would bother them. The rooms were plush, comfortable, and perfect for privacy.

"Good morning," she cooed as she opened the door and walked in. She stopped solidly in her tracks as she took in the six-foot, five-inch, salt-and-pepper haired stunner in front of her wearing a rich, navy-blue power suit minus the boring tie. It must have shown on her face that she was surprised at how hot he was because he laughed with a deep baritone chuckle.

"My God, woman," he said. "You're as gorgeous as Grace promised. Jesus, look at you."

Annnnd just like that, her pussy was soaking wet and ready for action. She didn't say that, of course. She wasn't running a hot house. This was a respectable salon and she'd never crossed that line as much as she'd wanted to. But this man…good Lord. She could think of one hundred lines she'd cross with him. *Get a hold of yourself.*

"You're a silver-tongued little devil, aren't you?" she said. She closed the door and the room suddenly felt very small. His one-thousand-dollar pants quickly became tight in his crotch. "What are we doing for you today?"

They both grinned at each other as the sexual undertones took hold and the heat started to rise between them.

"What's available?" he asked smoothly. She noticed his chiseled jaw clench as he took in her ample breasts. His stormy gray eyes clouded with desire as he admired her size sixteen frame and its curves.

"Everything," she said silkily. His eyebrows sprung up in surprise. "That is, everything to do with your hair and skin care."

She smiled wickedly as he returned the favor.

"I like you," he said gruffly.

"I'm a fine wine, Mr…?"

"Brand. Tucker Brand."

"Mr. Brand." She said it slowly and with a deeper register of her voice.

"Mmm," he murmured. "You just get better with time, eh?"

"Eh?" She chuckled. "Are you Canadian?"

"I wish. Great fucking people,"
he said. "But no, I'm American. I
do deal in sports, though, so I
spend a lot of time in Canada and a
few other select countries."

"Hockey?" She finally started to
move, grabbing her gear and setting
up his chair.

"That's one, yes," he said. "You
like hockey?"

"Big, beautiful men beating each
other around at high speeds?" She
winked at him. "Is there anything
hotter?"

He took his time running his
eyes up and down her body before
he said, "I can think of a few
things."

Most women might blush from a
stare like that. She didn't. It only
spurred her on.

"Sit," she ordered. She pointed
at the chair as she leveled a
haughty eyebrow at him.

"Yes, ma'am."

He took off his coat slowly exposing a silky white shirt that clung to his firm, muscled chest, thick and wide. He rolled up his sleeves as he stared right in her eyes, then sat down gently and leaned back.

"Do whatever you want."

She caught the sexy tones in his voice and all she could think was she wanted to open up that firm place between his legs, take his cock in her mouth, then slide onto it and fuck him wildly and with abandon.

"What are you thinking?" he asked.

She felt heat rush up her throat when he caught her staring at his bulge and she gave him a startled, but appreciative smile. "I bet you can guess."

He grinned as he shifted his hips to relieve the pressure of that hard

cock pushing against the expensive
fabric.

"I bet I can."

"So," she said low and quiet. "A
trim today? Or something more?"

"A trim will be fine." He took in
a slow breath and smiled. It made
her so wet she could barely walk
for fear her juices would smack as
she moved.

He didn't really need much. He
obviously took care of himself. His
clean-shaven, short-cut salt and
pepper hair reflected that. There
were a few stray hairs around the
edges, and she guessed that's what
he wanted taken care of. They were
small and barely noticeable, but he
was likely the type of man who
paid attention to such details, as did
she. There wasn't a hair on
Tabitha's body that was out of
place, including her freshly waxed
slit that was now dripping with
desire.

She stepped to him and started at the back, shockingly aware of her fingers and how they were touching him. Normally she was quick, getting clients in and out so they could get back to their life. With Tucker, she moved like her body was encased in sludge, dragging her fingers across his skin as she inhaled the fresh notes of soap and musk.

"Mmm," he moaned as she started to trim. "Your hands are so soft. They feel amazing."

She took a sharp breath as electric zapped through her body at his words. She wanted him. Damn, she wanted him.

"Everything on me is soft." Holy shit, did she just say that? She glanced at his pants, which were now ready to burst from the bulge underneath. *Oh shit, I did say it.*

"Oh really?" he teased.

She let out a low murmur as she moved to the front of him and started to trim. When he opened his legs so she could get closer, she stepped between them as though a magnet pulled her in. And when she felt his fingers start to trail up her inner thighs, she just kept cutting.

Oh, God, please touch me.

"You are soft," he whispered.

She closed her eyes as his fingers found her panties and slid underneath them. She breathed deeper and deeper as one finger slid into her wet pussy and then another.

"Mmm, Tabitha, you're so wet, baby," he said roughly. "Someday, I'm gonna slide my cock in that wetness and fuck you like crazy."

"Oh God," she said softly as she put her scissors down. His fingers massaged her pussy inside and out.

"You like that?" he asked.

She couldn't speak for the pleasure, so she just nodded as she felt her climax start to build low in her pelvis, right where his fingers were stroking her G-spot. It must have shown on her face because he asked, "Right there, Tabitha?"

"Yes." She nodded as she reached up and rubbed her breasts.

"Yes, baby, touch your titties, just like that," he said hotly. "Squeeze your nipples."

She did what he said and squeezed as his fingers rocked in and out of her slick folds.

"Oh God," she said breathlessly. "Yes."

"Right there?"

"Yes."

And now her climax was rounding the corner as his fingers slurped in and out of her pussy.

"Fuck me," she moaned.

"Yes, baby," he panted.

Suddenly he stopped, yanked her dress up, and dove into her wetness, tongue-first, eating her like she was his last meal.

"Tucker, yes!"

She could hear him licking and sucking and slurping as she grabbed his freshly cut hair and moved her pussy in time with his tongue.

"I'm gonna come," she panted. And she did. The strongest, fastest, most intense orgasm she'd ever had rocked her body in powerful waves over and over as his tongue danced on her clit.

"God, yes!"

She could barely control herself or her breathing as the orgasm took hold and then slowly released. She felt him pull away as she came down from the high. He stood and washed himself at the sink as she pulled her dress down with a smile.

He turned to face her with a wicked grin. "That was incredible."

"Yes," she said. "It was."

"Is that a special service you offer?"

"Look at me," she said. "I don't need it that bad, honey. You were my first."

"Mmmm, I haven't been anyone's first since I was sixteen."

She laughed. "And how old are you now?"

"Forty-six. And you?"

"Twenty-nine."

"And perfect."

"Such a smooth talker," she said.

"Can I talk you into dinner and drinks at my favorite bar tonight?" he asked. "I have a private room for dining."

"Just for dining?" she asked coyly.

He smiled.

"I think I can make that happen," she said.

"Good," he acknowledged. "I'll have my assistant send you the information. Say, seven?"

"Abso-fucking-lutely."

He laughed as he grabbed his jacket and headed for the door. "I fucking love a woman who knows how to talk dirty."

"Well, then," she said. "You'll fucking love me."

He opened the door and glanced over his shoulder with a wink. "Thanks for breakfast. It was delicious."

He looked at her pussy then back to her eyes. "See you later for dinner."

And with that he walked out. Tabitha's knees nearly buckled under the weight of that sexy grin, but she wasn't the type of woman to swoon over just anyone.

And as far as she could tell, Tucker Brand wasn't just anyone.

All she could think as she got hold of herself was: *Tucker-mother-fucker-Brand.*

3

And His Key

Tucker was by no means, nor by any modern relationship standard, a monogamous man. He was a playboy and he liked it. He had known since he was twenty years old that all he wanted was sex and women and money and that was it. He'd cut college classes at UCLA his junior year to go get a vasectomy and he felt like a million bucks when it was over.

He'd gone to a local bar and gobbled down a cheeseburger with a beer as he glanced at a tired man next to him and said, "I'm celebrating. I got a vasectomy today."

"Jesus," the guy had said. "I wish I'd thought o' that."

Tucker had laughed with
pleasure at his own cleverness.
Then a few years later, he said,
"fuck it," and got married. Wife
number one thought she could get
him to change his mind about kids.
When that didn't work, they got a
divorce. Wife number two thought
the same thing, which led to
divorce number two. If they wanted
children, they deserved them. It just
wasn't going to be with him.

He was a gentleman about it,
though, and he made sure he paid
them enough alimony to take care
of them for the rest of their lives in
the manner they were used to. It
wasn't, after all, their faults that he
was a sex-loving, son-of-a-bitch.
His boyish charm kept them from
hating him, but nothing could keep
them from continuing to love him
long after he left.

He loved them, too. He just
didn't want that bullshit "marriage

and kids" mirage clouding up his fucking life.

And now, there was Tabitha.

"Wow," he said to himself as he raised an eyebrow. He took a sip of his whiskey and smiled.

Tabitha was a dream boat with that sexy figure and breasts that made his mouth water. She tasted good, too, like sugar and spice. He especially liked the way she took care of herself. The details were tight, and he respected that.

"Mr. Brand?"

Tucker glanced to the hostess, a pretty twenty-something with a bright smile. "Yes?"

"Your dinner guest has arrived."

"Oh, please, send her in."

He stood and straightened his clothes, smoothed his hair, checked his breath. He felt nervous. And he hadn't felt nervous in a while. But there was something about Tabitha that made his heart beat a little faster.

He liked that, too.

"Holy fuck, woman," he said as she strode through the door. And boy did she walk into that room like a boss in her three-inch heels, body-hugging hot pink dress, and her short, blonde hair brushing her shoulders. *Fuck, that's hot.* "I like your brand, baby."

His eyes slid down her body, her calves, and to her heels. *I'm gonna leave those on.*

"My eyes are up here, asshole," she said sweetly.

He laughed at her brazenness as he gazed into her icy blue eyes. "You're right, I apologize."

He put one hand around her waist as he waved at the small booth with the other. "Our table for the evening."

He could tell she was impressed, but not too impressed. He liked

that, too. She knew what money
was, but she wasn't taken by it. An
important quality in a woman for a
man like him. He had stacks upon
stacks of money and sometimes,
women got carried away with that.

"This is gorgeous," she said. She
slid into the booth and slapped the
leather to invite him right next to
her.

"Damn, you're hot," he said. He
slid in right next to her and it took
only a minute for his hand to find
its place between her thighs at the
knee. He gave a squeeze. "How is a
lady like you available on a
moment's notice?"

"First of all, I'm not a lady," she
said coyly. "And second, I'm never
available on a moment's notice.
Except when I wanna be."

"A woman who knows what she
wants when she wants it," he said.

"Exactly."

The waiter walked up and poured them champagne, leaving the bottle in an ice bucket on the table.

"Dinner will be served shortly," he said. He gave a nod and left as they were alone once more.

Tucker peered at her. "I hope it's okay, the chef has decided to make us something special. Duck something. Are you good with that? Any allergies? Anything you hate? I'll take care of it."

She smiled as she took a sip of champagne. She gave him a sly grin. "I like to eat most anything."

Hot. Damn. He saw her gaze shift briefly to his cock, which was waking up and pushing itself against his pants once more. Anytime she walked in a room his nether regions suddenly had a mind of their own.

"You're excellent at innuendo," he said.

"I'm excellent at all of it."

He wanted to take her right then, but he thought better of it. He liked her and needed to know a bit more before he jumped in. And the way she looked in that dress…he wasn't going to last much longer before he bent her over the table and drove her pussy to the best orgasm she'd ever had.

"So, how long have you worked at Steel & Grace?" He took a sip of champagne to slow things down.

"Oh, honey." She laughed. "I own it. With Grace. I'm Steel. Tabitha Steel."

His dick got hard immediately. Not only was she sexy and gorgeous, and smart, but holy shit—she was a business owner with her own money. No wonder she took men who had it in stride.

"I'm fucking impressed," he said.

"You should be," she quipped. "I started with nothing. And I mean nothing. Grace and I built that salon to what it is today."

"Why hair and make-up?"

"Why not?" She gave him a sexy grin as she took a slow sip of champagne. He squeezed her knee and slowly rubbed her inner thigh. "No matter the economy, women and men always get their hair done. It's not recession-proof, of course, but it's more stoic than most."

"Damn woman, you're speaking my language." He slid his hand a little further up her thigh and her eyes blinked slowly as he massaged it.

"I also invest in the stock market," she said in a deep, raspy voice.

"Fuck." He moved in and took her mouth into a ravenous kiss as she responded in-kind. "I want you right now."

"Then fucking take me," she ordered.

"Fuck."

He stood quickly, pulling her up with him as the glasses and everything on the table tumbled to the floor in a fantastic fashion. She leaned over it, grabbing the other side.

"Fuck me!"

"Fuck yes," he moaned. He slid her dress up around her waist and sat down in the booth in front of her panty less pussy as he grabbed her ass and squeezed it. "You are a fucking delicious woman."

"Then eat me, baby," she moaned.

He dove right in, sliding his tongue up and down her slit as she groaned with pleasure.

"Yes," she breathed.

He loved eating pussy, but especially hers. Her folds were the perfect shade of pink and waxed to perfection. Her taste was both sweet and spicy and her wetness stayed on his tongue long enough for him to really taste her. The best part was that she loved it. Every time his tongue flicked her clit, she gripped the table. Every time he pushed into her wet hole, she moaned. She loved sex. And he loved that.

"Fuck me!"

"Whatever you want, baby," he said. He stood and as he unbuttoned his pants, she stood and turned to face him, dropping to her knees on the booth, and taking his hard cock deep in her throat.

"Oh fuck," he panted. "Yes. God, yes."

This was a woman who knew what she was doing and loved it. She teased his tip with her mouth and tongue while gripping his cock and stroking him. She licked and sucked his balls as he moaned and squeezed him with a pressure that made him want to come right there.

"Stop," he said. "I wanna fuck you."

She grinned and turned around, staying on her knees on the booth with her soaking wet pussy high and ready for him.

"Put that thick cock in me," she purred. She was a sex kitten and he loved it.

"You want this cock?"

"Yes, baby, please."

"Beg me," he ordered.

"Baby, slide your cock in me," she whimpered. "Please, baby, fuck me."

"Fuck." He couldn't hold back any longer as he teased her pussy with the tip before slamming that cock in her in one quick plunge.

"Yes!" she moaned.

Once he was fully in, God help him, he couldn't help but fuck her hard and fast.

"Harder, baby," she yelled with pleasure.

"You like that?"

"God, yes," she moaned. "Slap my ass, baby!"

He slapped her hard on the ass once, twice, three times, and she panted with pleasure.

"Again!"

He slapped her once more and pounded that wet, beautiful pussy until he could feel his orgasm gathering.

"I'm gonna come, baby," he moaned.

"I'm coming now," she screamed. "Yes!"

"Yes, baby, come!" He felt her body convulse with pleasure as she came. He quickly pulled out and came all over her lower back and pussy.

"Fuck," he said as his salty release painted her skin. "Fuck, you're beautiful."

"Mmm," she murmured. "Fuck,
that was good."

"Yeah, it was," he said. He
grabbed a napkin and cleaned her
off, then helped her stand, pulling
her dress down and helping her
clean up. He glanced at the smile
on her lips. "Fuck, you're
amazing."

"You're not so fucking bad
yourself."

He chuckled at her honesty. "I
didn't hurt you, did I? The
slapping. Your ass okay?"

"Oh, honey," she said with a
wink. "My ass is just fine."

He laughed again as the waiter
appeared, saw them, then turned
and walked away. He turned back
to Tabitha and they both laughed.

"Let me go talk to him and see if
dinner is about ready."

"That sounds wonderful," she
said. "I'm starving. And I'll clean
this up."

He started to walk away but then the thought struck him that she may the kind of woman who would like other things he had to offer in his life. Like his club. His…special club.

"Tabitha?"

"Yeah," she said. She quit straightening up to look at him.

"I have a membership to a…unique club here in town. Would you like to join me sometime?"

"Unique?" she asked curiously. "What the fuck does that mean?"

He grinned. "I'll explain when I come back."

And he hoped once he enlightened her, she'd be up for the club's distinctive flavor of fun.

4

Go or Don't Go

Tabitha stared at the key card on her nightstand and remembered the way it felt for Tucker to take her at dinner not once, but twice. She was a lover of sex and always with partners who could fuck well and please her. Tucker certainly had fulfilled that requirement.

But something else was nagging at her. *I think I might like that fucker.*

"Fuck," she hissed to no one as she sat up on her plush, King-sized bed, naked and wet from her shower. How could she let herself like that sexy bastard?

She smiled as she thought of him and his arrogant confidence, the way he took charge, and the

maddening way he made her feel
like she was the only woman in the
room. Except she knew better than
to think she was the only woman or
could ever be. Tucker was the male
version of her, and she would never
ask him to give that life up.

She glanced at the key again.
And then he gave her that damn
key card.

"It's a sex club," he had said.
"I'd like you to come with me
tomorrow night. I promise…you'll
love it."

She'd heard of the club he was
talking about. It was high-end,
clean as a whistle, and was open to
every fantasy its members could
imagine. It was the kind of club
membership only money could
buy, and a place she'd always
wanted to try.

And now she had a key. His key.

"Meet me there at eight," he had
said.

"I'll think about it," she had
replied. And then he fucked her so
good she thought she might never
come down from the high.

The memory made her start to
ache between her thighs. She
reached into her side drawer and
pulled out her favorite sex toy, the
most perfect dildo with a vibrating
clit massager that hit her in just the
right spot. She was already wet just
from thinking about Tucker and
needed to take the edge off if she
was going to go.

And she *was* going to go. She
already knew that the minute he
handed her the key. Everything
since then was the "good girl"
voice in her head trying to convince
her otherwise.

She was not convinced.

She chuckled as she spread her
legs and rubbed her breasts softly
before moving down her stomach
to her pussy and touching herself. It

felt so good to have her own hands
between her legs.

"Mmm," she murmured as she
grabbed her dildo and slid it deep
inside her. "Fuck."

She thought about Tucker and
his magnetic smile, and the way it
felt when he had kissed down her
throat and massaged her breasts.

"Suck my nipples," she'd
ordered him."

"Fuck yes," he had groaned. He
had taken her nipple in his mouth
and sucked it slow, licking one
while he squeezed the other. Then
he'd trade off.

The memory made her pussy
grip her dildo tightly as it rubbed
against her G-spot. She turned on
the clit massager and it jolted her
pleasure to ten as she felt her
orgasm rising in her pelvis.

"Fuck," she moaned. Tucker had
the most magnificent cock, too, so
thick it filled her to the edges,

pushing against her walls with force every time he moved inside of her.

She thrust the dildo harder inside of her pussy as the thought of his cock made her reach the brink.

"Yes, yes!"

The clit massager rung her bell as her orgasm flowed through her body at a quick pace making her catch her breath.

"Fuck yes," she said as she pulled out the cock and set it beside her.

"Not as good as Tucker," she whispered. "But damn close."

She smiled to herself and glanced sideways to her closet. She had to choose what to wear tonight.

"So many options," she sighed as she got up and started to flip through the delicately hanging numbers.

Whatever she decided on, she knew one thing: It needed to make

Tucker want to come in his pants as
soon as he saw her.

5

Fantasies Revealed

Tucker waited by the door of the club slowly sipping his whiskey as he people-watched. The club was filled with beautiful women tonight, a few of which he'd already decided he wanted to fuck. There was the brunette in the blue dress and the blonde in the green, low-cut top. He was also considering the redhead on the bed in the back. The last time he'd seen her, though, she was being eaten out by a guy he knew at the stock market. He hated that fucking guy, so, as gorgeous as she was, it was unlikely he'd fuck her after that prick.

Fuck, I'm nervous.

He drained the remaining whiskey and put the glass down on

a passing tray as he watched the door open and close as another woman who wasn't Tabitha passed by.

What was it about her, anyway? He couldn't quite put his finger on it, but he'd fucked, and married, enough women to know it wasn't just sex with this gorgeous fucking goddess. What exactly it was, he didn't know, but he was sure as shit going to enjoy finding out.

"Tabitha," he whispered as she finally walked through the door. "Fuck."

He probably could have come in his pants right then and there if there hadn't been twenty people standing nearby. Her curves were wrapped in a black leather dress that was made of what looked like leather bandages at the top. Her hair was in a 1950s wave that framed her beautiful face and her

pouty lips were bright red and
ready for action.

She looked like a mother-
fucking pin-up girl for a bondage
magazine as she moved like a
panther toward him. His cock paid
attention and reported for duty:
Hard and at the ready. As she
reached him, she slid her hand
between his legs and grabbed it
firmly as she gazed in his eyes.

"Glad to see you're ready for
tonight."

"Holy fuck," he panted.

"Me, too," she quipped. She
smiled, let go of his cock, and
strode into the club with purpose.

Fuck. Me.

He turned and followed her like
a lost puppy as they headed to the
bar. He got the bartender's
attention and ordered them both
whiskey on the rocks. As the
bartender made their drinks, he

looked her over. She was absolutely fucking beautiful.

"So," she said. "How exactly does this place work?"

He smiled. He loved that he was showing her something new and that it was with him. The novelty was exhilarating.

"Well, most members come here with something sexual they want to try already in their mind," he said. "Then, when they get here, they can usually find like-minded people who want to share that same fantasy pretty quickly."

"What do you like when you're here?"

He grinned as the bartender set their drinks down. He grabbed hers and handed it to her. "I like a few things."

He glanced around then back to her. "Threesomes are fun. Sometimes it's just sex with someone new. I like women who like a little bondage sometimes."

He saw her eyes start that slow blink that meant she was getting turned on.

"Am I making you wet?" he whispered.

She nodded as she sipped her drink.

"What did *you* come here for tonight?" he asked.

She swallowed the cool, brown liquid down her throat and looked right in his eyes. "You."

His cock jumped and saluted at the look in her eyes, getting immediately hard at the desire pulsing from her body.

"Tie me up," she ordered. "And invite whoever you want to join in."

He took her drink from her and set it on the bar beside his as he took her hand and led her back the twisted hallways to his personal

VIP room. He swiped his card and the private door opened. He nodded at the concierge standing next to it and whispered to go find the brunette and blonde, and send them back, along with their dates.

As the man hurried away, Tucker led Tabitha into the opulent room, filled with toys, plenty of surfaces for fucking, and a fridge full of water, Gatorade, and fruit.

"No alcohol?" she asked as she glanced at the fridge.

"Call me old-fashioned," he said as he smiled at her. "But I happen to think women should make decisions about sex while sober and informed. I never have alcohol in here. No drugs, either. Those are hard and fast rules."

"Good rules," she said.

He could see the desire in her eyes as she dropped her purse, slipped over to him, and kissed him deeply as his body responded with pleasure. She smelled like the most erotic scent of vanilla he could imagine, and her curves felt soft and silky under his grip.

"You're amazing, Tabitha," he whispered.

"So are you, handsome," she said. She ripped his shirt open, and he lost all sense of control as he gripped her throat gently and kissed her passionately.

"Yes," she panted.

He grabbed the zipper on the back of her dress and slid it down her back as she helped him pull it off her.

"Oh fuck," he whispered. Her pale skin was beautiful in this light and her breasts were heavy and gorgeous. Her curves were like a goddess sent from the heavens with the most perfectly shaped ass he'd ever seen. "Tabitha."

She put her finger on his lips as she undressed him, laying a trail of

kisses from his neck to his belly.
She lightly pushed him backward
onto the bed as the door opened. As
she straddled him, the two couples
walked through the door and
started undressing each other.

They took in the sight of Tabitha
stroking his hard cock and started
stripping each other of their
clothes. Tucker glanced to Tabitha
to make sure she was okay, but
before he could look in her eyes, he
felt her hot, wet pussy slide onto
his cock.

"Oh my God," she moaned.
"This is so hot."

He watched her intensely as she
rode him like a pro while eagerly
watching the couples as they
started to fuck.

"Fuck yes," she murmured.

"Fuck me harder," he ordered.

"Yes, baby," she said. She
glanced at the couples again,
settling on the brunette. That was

his favorite, too. "I want her titties in my mouth."

He almost came when she said that, but he held tight. He caught the brunette's stare and nodded her over. As she got to them, Tabitha reached out and pulled the woman to her.

"Fuck, yes," he panted. Tabitha kissed the brunette and then slid the woman's perky breasts into her mouth. Tucker reached out and grabbed the brunette's hips, gently pulling her pussy to him. She took the hint and climbed on, putting her ass and pussy in his face while she and Tabitha licked and kissed each other's titties.

"I'm gonna come," Tabitha moaned.

"Come, baby," he said.

"Oh God, yes!" she cried out.

He could feel Tabitha's pussy squirm and tighten all over his cock as she came. He came, too, with the beautiful brunette's pussy in his mouth while Tabitha came on his stiff cock.

The blonde's husband came calling for the brunette and lifted her up, slamming her against the wall and fucking her while his own wife got fucked by the other woman's husband. He took in the pleasure on Tabitha's face.

"You like it?" he asked.

"I love it," she said.

"Want more?"

She nodded with a smile.

"I'll give you as much as you want," he said assuredly.

"Good," she said. "Then tell me: what the fuck are you waiting for?"

6

Work and Play

Tabitha didn't realize she was humming a tune until Grace pointed it out.

"I'm begging you, stop," the petite powerhouse chirped from her private station in the central part of the salon. Grace was sporting a slick black look today in black heels, black leggings and a black, oversized long-sleeved shirt. Her hair was pulled into a ponytail and her silver and turquoise jewelry sparkled.

"I didn't know I was fucking doing it," Tabitha smirked. Then she winked at Grace. "But I have good reason to."

"Does this have to do with smokin' hot Tucker Brand?"

Tabitha grinned as she smoothed down her cream-colored, fitted sweater that fell over the black leggings she was sporting and knee-high boots. "It might."

"I want details," she said as a bell dinged. Grace glanced to the door. "After my client."

Grace sped away as Tabitha went back to readying her work station for the day, humming a tune as she went. She barely heard the second ding of the door—but she definitely heard the low baritone rumble of Tucker's voice when he asked for her.

She peeked in the mirror at her appearance and slid on some bright lipstick as she grinned with approval. She stepped back and started to sashay toward the front when she stopped cold in her tracks.

"Hi," he said. His sleek gray suit was fitted perfectly against his chiseled frame. "You remember Paula."

On Tucker's arm was the brunette from the club, dressed to the nines in a stunning wrap dress and heels while grinning from ear to ear. Tabitha could tell by the look on both of their faces that he had intended this as a good surprise, but that's not how it felt. She must have carried that emotion on her face because he quickly frowned and asked Paula to wait for him in the car.

As Paula walked out, Tucker walked toward her. "Tabitha?"

"Why the fuck would you bring her here?" she hissed quietly. "This is my place of business. I fucking own this salon. People fucking know me here."

She twisted on her toe and whipped around toward the private area as he quickly followed.

"Tabitha, wait, I'm sorry," he said apologetically. She could hear his footsteps closing in behind her as they reached the private room where they first met. She ran in first and he quickly followed, shutting the door behind him.

"Holy shit, I'm so sorry," he said. He took a step toward her as she held out her hand for him to stop. He did. "I thought it would be fun. To come here, tease you a little, and then meet up later."

"Why would that be fun, Tucker? Here, this salon, this is my world. The club, that's a separate world. Those two things are not to be combined," she spat.

"Does that include me, too? I'm in the other world?"

She glared at him. "What did you think was gonna happen, Tucker? You'd bring her here and we'd do it in a threesome in the private room? I told you, you were the first and only for me here. And it will never happen again, by the way. I don't mix business with pleasure, ever."

She looked him over as he raised an eyebrow at her.

"You were my exception," she sighed.

"So, I was a mistake, then?"

"Of course not," she said quietly. "But you bringing her here most certainly was."

He sighed as he shoved his hands in his pockets. "I said I was sorry. I meant it. Now, how can I fix it?"

"You want to fix it?" she asked earnestly.

"Of course," he answered. "Tabitha, I like you. Genuinely."

"I like you, too," she said.

They shared a little smile.

He shrugged as he looked her over. "I didn't expect you."

"Well, I didn't expect you, either."

He smiled as he walked toward her. "So does this mean you forgive my idiocy?"

"I fucking suppose." She shrugged as he slid his arms around her waist and pulled her to him.

"Listen, here's the deal with me," he said. "I don't ever want to get married again. I also don't want to be monogamous. I like having sex, I love the club, it's who I am."

"I know that," she said. She slid her hands up his arms. "I completely understand it.

"But…fuck woman." He dragged his eyes over her body, landing on her stare. "You're giving me the feels."

She laughed as he dove in and kissed her neck.

"You're not so fucking bad yourself."

He kissed her before taking a step back. He asked: "Do you have a proposal for how we should proceed?"

"Well, to start, don't ever fucking mix business with pleasure again," she said. She winked at him. "You were a one-time deal. No more."

He nodded. "Okay, I respect that."

"I also love sex and have no intention of settling down. Having said that…" she paused and grinned at him. "I wouldn't mind spending time with just you. As long as we both know we're not fucking monogamous."

"Okay, I fucking like that," he said. "So, we'd spend some time just us then?"

She nodded. "Absolutely."

"And some time with a few other people?"

"Oh, definitely," she said. She kissed him deeply.

"Well, let me make up for my bad behavior today then," he said. He winked at her. "Can you get the weekend free?"

She nodded. "I can and I fucking will."

"Good," he said. "I'll pick you up tomorrow at noon for the weekend."

He kissed her once more and turned to leave.

"What should I pack?"

He turned and ran his eyes up and down her body. "Absolutely fucking nothing, gorgeous."

He winked as he walked out the door and she swore she felt something like feelings bubbling up in her belly.

7

The More of You, the Better

Tabitha stood at the wall of windows and stared at Lake Erie as the sun set. The beautiful golds and pinks made the view look like a postcard as the lake churned and sparkled at the sandy shore.

"This is fucking stunning," she said quietly as she sipped her tequila.

"You're stunning," he said softly. He walked up behind her and slid his arms around her waist. He gently kissed her neck then nuzzled into the crook of it as he slowly swayed with her body to the quiet tunes of Michael Buble on the house's surround sound.

"This is perfect." She kissed his forehead as she slid her free hand up his forearm.

He sighed as they stayed like that for a moment. "I haven't felt like this in a while," he murmured into her neck. "It feels nice."

"It does, doesn't it?" she quipped. She hadn't felt like this ever. She knew she wasn't in love with him, but she also didn't want to fuck him and leave, either. That was new for her.

Tabitha had a deep appreciation for her sexual partners and always maintained a positive post-sex relationship. Sometimes it led to more sex, but it never led to more relationship.

She was a one-woman show, building her business empire with a soon-to-release second location in Columbus, followed by Cincinnati and then expanding into the region by way of Chicago, New York, and eventually, Toronto. She had big dreams, and she didn't want those interrupted by small relationships.

But Tucker was different. There was nothing—absolutely nothing—small about Tucker. His life was big. From his four thousand square-foot lake house and million-dollar bank account to his investment portfolios and that perfectly shaped cock.

And because of that, he understood her in a way many men didn't. He got her, supported her big dreams, and he didn't flinch in the face of them. More than that, he understood her desire to play and not settle down. At least not yet, or maybe ever. He was willing to explore what that could mean in terms of, what she was now considering, a different kind of relationship—perhaps, an open one?

"Tucker, can we talk?"

He pulled away as she turned to face him. "Of course, beautiful. Hit me."

"You already know I'm a very direct person, so I'd like to just be fucking open about where we're at right now."

He chuckled. "I'd expect nothing less."

"Good." She sipped her tequila and peered at him over the rim as the thick liquor cascaded down her throat. "I'd like to date you. And I'd like for it to be an open relationship. At least for now. How do you feel about that?"

He smiled as he shoved his hands in his pocket. "So, you're proposing we date, as normal couples might date, get to know each other and spend time together as a couple, but we're also free to date other people?"

She nodded. "Yes, just like that."

"What about sex?"

"The more of you, the better," she retorted.

His eyes lit with humor as a small laugh escaped his chest. "I meant, with other people."

"You mean, the two of us plus other people? Or do you mean, other sexual relationships outside of this one?"

"How about both?" he asked with a little shrug.

She thought about that for a moment. She definitely had a cascade of jealousy when she saw him with that brunette, so she wasn't entirely sure she'd be able to handle if he was having sex with other women outside of their relationship. But, if she wasn't going to limit herself, she couldn't limit him.

"I'm definitely open to the club and its multi-partner benefits, so long as it's safe, protected sex," she said earnestly. "I'm not sure where I'm at on the other relationship aspect just yet. Are you?"

"I actually am," he said. "I'd prefer to focus on getting to know *you*. I can't do that if I'm getting to know someone else at the same time."

A heated moment passed between them as he stepped to her and put his hands on her waist. He gazed into her eyes.

"I'm not saying we're committed, Tabitha. I'm just saying, how about we take a couple months and focus on getting to know each other?" He gave her waist a squeeze. "We can enjoy the club and its benefits, and each other, and then we can revisit this conversation again in a few months, after the New Year."

Her stomach churned with butterflies as she gazed into his beautiful, gray eyes. She could tell

he was sincere. And she agreed
with all of it, giving him a little
nod.

"Good," he said softly. "Until
then, I'll restrict my sexual and
romantic partners to just you and I,
plus what we experience together at
the club. And we'll see how that
goes. How does that sound to
you?"

She put her glass down on a
small table behind the large, oversized couch, then ran her hands up
his arms and around his neck. As
she did, he pulled her in tight and
gave her a light kiss.

"I'd like that," she said. She
kissed him as he slid his hands up
her back. "And I'd like to show you
just how much I like it."

"Mmm, yes, please," he cooed.

"You haven't seen my softer
side yet," she cooed back.

He shook his head slowly. "No,
but I'd like to."

A smile passed between them as her gut reacted with something more gentle and caring than she was used to. She couldn't say she was falling for him, but she couldn't say she wasn't, either. There was just simply a warm, lovely feeling brewing inside her that made her want to touch him differently than any other man who had crossed her path.

"Come," she directed as she let go of him, took only his hand, and then led him to the bedroom.

"Only if you do." He grinned at her when she glanced over her shoulder.

As they walked the plush, cream carpet of the hallway to the bedroom, her whole body relaxed into the new feelings buzzing through her body. She felt safe with Tucker and taken care of. She didn't need him to take care of her, of course, she had her own money, her own place, her own life, but she couldn't deny how positively lovely it felt to know he *could* take care of her if she needed him to.

"You're quiet," he noted as they stepped into the bedroom, soaked in the golden glow of sunset.

She let go of his hand and turned to face him. She said nothing as she slowly unbuttoned her fitted, white button-down, then slid it off her body, revealing a lacy white bra that held her D-cup breasts in a provocative, stunning way.

"Jesus," he murmured. The fabric in his crotch started to tighten as his cock grew at the sight of her.

"Sit down," she ordered, turning to face the bed. He did as he was told and sat in front of her, taking his own shirt off as he did. He reached out to touch her and she slapped his hand. "Not yet."

He smiled as she stepped back
and unhooked her pencil skirt. She
slowly slipped it off her body,
revealing a matching lacy thong.

"Mmm," he moaned. He reached
between his legs and rubbed his
cock.

"That's my job," she purred.

She stepped between his legs
and took his hand off his cock, then
dropped to her knees in front of
him.

"Tabitha," he moaned as she un-
did his pants and gently released
his hard cock from its cage. "Yes.
God, yes."

She took the tip of his gorgeous
manhood into her mouth and
sucked like it was the most
delicious popsicle she'd ever tasted
in her life.

"Oh fuck." She smiled as he
tipped his head back in pleasure,
groaning when she swallowed him
deeper. "Tabitha."

She loved oral sex, there was no doubt about it. Having a man in your mouth and giving him pleasure beyond his wildest dreams was one of her most favorite things. That feeling was only enhanced with Tucker. She wanted to make him feel as good as he made her feel.

"You're so amazing, beautiful," he panted.

She swallowed him all the way down her throat, taking his balls gently into her hand as she did.

"Oh God," he moaned.

She stayed there for a minute just swallowing and sucking and fondling him. It felt good to have him on the brink, to know she was giving him an intense amount of pleasure.

"Tabitha, stop or I'll come, please."

She pulled back, letting him slide out of her mouth, but not before swallowing the tip again and gripping his shaft tightly as she rubbed him.

"Oh fuck," he said as he sat up and looked in her eyes. "Baby, fuck."

She let go of him again and this time licked the shaft and tip like a dripping ice cream cone. "I love your cock, baby."

"Fuck."

"It's so perfect and delicious." She quickly swallowed his whole cock again as a moan burst from his chest.

"Holy fucking shit, I'm gonna come."

He reached down and slid his hands in her hair as she swallowed him down and held him there.

"Baby, I'm gonna come," he said urgently. She could tell he was giving her a chance to pull back so she wouldn't have to swallow, but the thing was, she wanted to

swallow his salty release. Wanted
to drink it down with his beautiful
cock.

Once he realized that, he grinned
and gripped her head while gently
rocking his cock into her mouth.
"Fuck, I'm coming."

His cock pulsed as he came long
and hard down her throat, the
waves of pleasure rocking his
whole body as he moaned.

"Tabitha, fuck, yes."

When she was sure he was done,
she slowly sucked and licked his
cock as she let him out of her
mouth, taking care to clean him and
kiss him as she did. Once it was
out, she gently kissed and stroked
his balls, his cock, his lower
stomach, and thighs.

When he was totally relaxed, she
leaned back and smiled.

"Woman, you're somethin'
fuckin' else," he said. He leaned
forward and gently took her face in

his hands, giving her a light kiss. "I can't wait to jump in this thing with you."

"Me, too," she said quietly. He gently kissed her again.

"Now," he said, standing up and offering her his hand. She took it and stood as he slid his arms around her. "It's my turn to show you how I feel about you."

He let go and walked out of the room.

"What the fuck?" she whispered under her breath.

She heard him rustling around, then the music clicked off and back on as Etta James' "At Last," spilled softly from the house speakers. Her lips twitched up in a soft grin as he walked back in wearing nothing but a sexy smile and a yellow diamond bauble on his index finger.

She gasped as she stared at the sparkler.

"Tabitha," he said as he closed the distance and stood in front of her, now holding the yellow diamond in his hand. "This is a beautiful promise to fuck you as hard and as good you want for as long as you want, baby."

She laughed and nodded as he slipped the ring on the middle finger of her right hand.

"Oh, Tucker," she said as she flipped him off. "I fucking love it, baby."

"Yeah ya do." He pulled her into a slow dance. "You're fucking amazing, baby. One of a kind. Just like that fucking diamond."

She laughed as he slowly twirled her in the amber light that was headed for evening.

"I fucking know, right?" she said enthusiastically as she eyed its beauty.

He laughed as he pulled her close and they danced slowly and intimately. He gave her a gentle kiss.

"Here's to getting to know each other better and seeing what this fucking is, eh?"

She nodded then touched her forehead to his.

"Fuck yes," she whispered.

And for the first time in her life, she had something other than sex with a man.

She had a relationship.

8

What Happens Next?

"I don't…" Annie shook her head.

"I'm literally stunned," Summer quipped.

"I'm trying to summon the words," Fawn said. "But there are none."

Tabitha grinned as the three sets of eyes drilled holes into her. She shrugged with joy at rendering her friends speechless.

"I fucking know, right?" Tabitha squealed. "Tucker-mother-fucker-Brand."

She shook her head with delight just thinking about him as she held her right hand in front of her and admired the diamond once more.

"So, wait," Annie said. "So, it is
monogamous, or it isn't?"

Tabitha shrugged as she dropped
her hand back in her lap. "It's both
for now. We're monogamous in the
sense we're not seeing anyone else
so we can know each other better.
But we're also enjoying sex at the
club with other partners to meet the
other sexual needs we enjoy."

"And you trust that he's not
sleeping with anyone else?" Fawn
asked.

"I trust he's not sleeping with
anyone else outside of the club,
yes," she said. "He has no reason to
lie. We're totally fucking honest
with each other about our sexual
needs. And, we're not saying it's
forever, we're saying it's for a few
months until we can see what it is."

"Total honesty, huh?" Summer
asked. "I like it.

"I can say from experience, it
only works with total honesty when

there are multiple people involved," Annie said. "Traditional relationships are hard. Non-traditional ones are even harder and take a lot more communication. Sounds like you've got that."

Tabitha appreciated Annie's point of view.

"It really fucking does, right?"

Annie nodded. "You have to go for it, Tabitha," she said. "You won't know unless you give it a try. If it works, and there's something more there, great. If it doesn't, at least you tried. I think it's amazing that you've found someone you can feel more for than just sex."

"Yeah, right there with you on that one," Summer said. "Tabitha, you'll never be a traditional person. To find a guy who can support that, and explore a different kind of relationship with you, and be honest about it, I mean. Priceless."

"I agree, Tabs," Fawn said. "I'm so happy to see you happy and feeling something special for someone else like this. How does it feel for you?"

Tabitha sipped her tequila as she thought about that.

"It feels weird and wonderful," she said. "I wasn't sure I was fucking capable. Now, I know I am. It's fucking lovely."

They all laughed as Tabitha gave a little shrug.

"Maybe it'll be something, maybe it won't, but, ladies," she said as she leaned forward. "What a beautiful mother-fucking ride to be on."

"Cheers to that!" Fawn said as she raised the last of her juice.

"Salute!" Summer added as she raised her drink.

"Salute!" Annie said, her glass in the air.

"Bitches, yes," Tabitha said as she raised the last of her tequila. "To feelings that involve more than just sex. God love 'em and the hormones they produce."

The ladies laughed as their glasses clinked and the beautiful fall morning warmed into a sunny afternoon.

<u>**More to Come!**</u>

Tabitha's love story isn't over! Keep reading the *Girls Who Brunch Erotic Series* to see what happens to Tabitha and Tucker! Wanna learn more about the other ladies—Annie, Fawn, and Summer? Keep reading the *Girls Who Brunch Erotic Series* as they have brunch, enjoy sex, and talk about it all!

Scan me

<u>**Want to read more?**</u>

Follow Author Lacey Love below
to get notifications every time a
new book is released. Want to learn
more about our other erotic series
Men Who Renovate? Then head to
workingbluepress.com!

Scan me